IN THE SHADOW OF THE
Striker

David Clayton
Illustrated by Trevor Parkin

OXFORD
UNIVERSITY PRESS

OXFORD
UNIVERSITY PRESS

Great Clarendon Street, Oxford OX2 6DP

Oxford University Press is a department of the University of Oxford.
It furthers the University's objective of excellence in research, scholarship,
and education by publishing worldwide in

Oxford   New York

*Athens Auckland Bangkok Bogotá Buenos Aires Cape Town
Chennai Dar es Salaam Delhi Florence Hong Kong Istanbul Karachi
Kolkata Kuala Lumpur Madrid Melbourne Mexico City Mumbai Nairobi
Paris São Paulo Shanghai Singapore Taipei Tokyo Toronto Warsaw*

with associated companies in *Berlin Ibadan*

Oxford is a registered trade mark of Oxford University Press in the UK and
in certain other countries

ISBN 0 19 919272 3

CHAPTER 1

Joe Jackson, star striker

It's funny, isn't it? One minute you're skimming along and the sun is shining and the next you're tumbling down a black hole and you don't know where you'll end up.

No, wait a minute! I've told you three lies already. I've never skimmed along at anything. The sun wasn't shining much in *my* head on the Saturday I'm talking about, and there was nothing surprising about things going wrong at our house.

Something happened between my mum and dad a long time ago and that's that. I just built a wall in my head called 'football' and hoped that some day all the trouble would go away. But life isn't that easy, is it?

Anyway, one Saturday last December, everything fell to pieces and this is what happened.

It was a special day for me, City were playing United and I had a ticket, thanks to my mate Nosher who had a spare. You can get tickets for usual games for ten Mars bar wrappers – but at Christmas? And against United? No way!

You might think that I'd be up at dawn, bouncing with excitement, but I wasn't. I was very tired. The night before, Mum had come in very late and Dad wasn't happy about it.

So, in the morning, instead of being up and getting my stuff together, I was lying in bed with my head superglued to the pillow.

'Sean? *Sean*? Are you getting up or not?' The low quiet voice of Suzie, my twin sister, was buzzing in my ear. 'Dad is making some breakfast. It's nearly ten o'clock!'

I was about to say something when she said, 'Shhhhh! Don't wake Mum!' and slipped away.

I whipped on my City shirt and stumbled downstairs to humour Dad.

The air in the kitchen was thick with blue smoke, smelling of burnt toast and charred bacon. Dad shuffled in with a face like a wet cod and clattered the burnt sacrifice on to my plate.

'Hey, Dad! Can I have mine medium-burned?' I asked, but he didn't smile.

When Dad turned away to burn more bacon, Suzie pointed upstairs and put a finger to her lips.

I shrugged.

She did a throat-slitting motion.

'I'm off to the match soon,' I said.

Suzie gave me a hard look.

'What have I done now?' I said.

'I'm going to be stuck here on my own! Claire and Anna have gone to London. I want to go with you.'

'You can't today,' I said. 'It's all ticket. Sorry!'

'Well, I'm off to Gran's then!'

'Any other day, you could come with me but . . .'

It sounded like I was making excuses, but it was true. And there was no way that I was going to miss the match. Football is everything to me, a lighthouse shining through the week from Saturday to Saturday.

I slipped up to my room and locked the door quietly.

There, Giant Joe Jackson, City's star striker, my idol, stared down at me from the wall tuning my mind to football. As I looked at the poster, I could hear the thunder of the crowd at Platt Field and my mind flew across the city to the stadium where I would stand with twenty thousand others in blue shirts feeling good, feeling part of things.

Today was 'the big one' – City against United, bottom against top, underdog against champions. A massive, tattered City flag filled half my wall like a battle standard. I liked City. They were sort of human and they never gave up, not like United, all money and flash and power.

'Today *we* win, eh, Joe?' I said. Joe stared on. Joe never smiled.

Dad couldn't bear the mention of his name, never knew why. But then, Dad wasn't interested in football. He hardly ever came to watch me play. Sometimes he didn't even seem to notice whether I was playing or not. But I didn't much care. It was just normal.

Ten-thirty. Time to lay out my match gear on the bed: money, scarf, baseball cap and air-horn. Not much to remember, but I never liked taking chances and checked things again and again. Then there was Sunday's kit to get ready. Joe isn't the only one who plays football. I, Sean Connor, had a vital game in Vernon Park for Park Villa under-15s the day after. I, too, was a striker, top scorer in the league actually, behind Tony Street. Tony went to my school and nobody ever scored more than Tony.

As I folded my gear, I glanced out of the window. There, far away, City's ground rose like a white whale high on the far side of the river and, beyond it, dark clouds were coming, running like a steel curtain across the sky.

Time to go. I slipped away silently, but just as I opened the front door, there was a sound behind me. I froze but it was Dad. He held a finger to his lips and pressed something in my hand. It was a crumpled tenner. It wasn't like him to give me money, especially to watch Joe.

'Hey, thanks, Dad!' I gasped.

Then, as the door closed, I raced for freedom. Far away, the great silver lights of the stadium glittered in the sun. Round the corner, I gave a shout and punched the air. Yehhhh! City here I come! If only I was you, Joe! If only . . . !

CHAPTER 2

Nosher

On United's home days, the road to town is a red flood of scarves and shirts and banners. When City play, the human river is blue. In the city centre, the fans form a swirling whirlpool of sound and colour and that was where I was due to meet Nosher and his valuable ticket.

He was standing by a fast-food stall, stuffing a hot dog down his throat whilst some spotty, United skinheads amused themselves at his expense. 'Hey, lads, look what the wind's blown along – Nellie the Blue Elephant!'

Nosher tucked his blue scarf into his coat. He

was so glad to see me that he splattered me with tomato sauce. He's all style, that kid.

I glanced at my watch. Almost time for the football special, a bus direct to the ground.

'Oh, look, he's got a keeper now!' The skins closed in. Any time now there would be trouble. We were big but they were bigger.

'Let's go, Nosh,' I said dragging him along.

'Isn't there time for another –' As he spoke, a half-eaten hot dog smacked against the back of his neck.

'Come on!' I said urgently. 'Never mind stuffing yourself!'

Nosh followed, looking over his shoulder every two seconds. Soon we were in the City queue. United skins here? You must be joking! Some of the City supporters are hard boys too.

Dark clouds swept across the town and fine, icy rain needled into us. But the atmosphere at the bus station was fantastic. There were about twelve bus queues. We were on one side, United were on the other. In between was a cordon of guys from the bus company and police. Nobody stepped out of line.

'You're a load of rubbish!' we chanted.

'You're going DOWNNNNN CITY!' back they came.

'MONEYBAGS, MONEYBAGS, HAHAHA!!!'

The chants got louder and louder.

Finally, we were on the bus.

CI-TEH!!! BOOM-BOOM-BOOM! Our feet were thundering on the floor. The driver didn't come upstairs. We were on our way and I was flying. No Mum, no Dad, no skinheads, no school! We were CI-TEH! That was all that mattered.

We reached City's ground at last – snakes of crowds, hustling policemen, hot dog smoke and tinny pop music swirling over the wall. Then came the pushing and pressing and squeezing outside the gates.

I saw Joe's black Jaguar with the big striker in it. He wasn't smiling. His face was set hard, full of concentration. The papers said he was in trouble, what with getting divorced again and a couple of car smashes. But what did they know? He was our Joe!

Then BAM! we were through the turnstile and inside, where the music was terrible and the grease-ball pies even worse. But, did I care? No. I loved this other world, my scruffy, noisy, football world. CI-TEH! CI-TEH!

In thirty minutes, I'd see Joe Jackson again and United would be shaking in their boots.

We were half-way up behind the goal at the City end.

UNI-TED! UNI-TED! The other end was thundering. Their boots didn't sound very shaky right then.

They were them and we were us: two tribes,
two worlds. They went to matches to win. We
went to have a go. The match would decide who
was best.

CHAPTER 3

City!

The match began and United played with their fans and the wind behind them. They started fast.

The red wave rolled in like a hurricane with the dark sky above and in front, the sandy, frozen beach of our penalty area. We could see the storm coming but we couldn't do anything about it.

From the first kick, things got worse and worse. In no time at all, they were camped out in our goal area. Please don't score! I prayed. And they didn't – at first. Ten men played back for us with big Joe all alone up front. A sort of 1-9-1 plan, if you can call a desperate struggle a plan.

I don't remember the details. It's all a horrible blur. I just remember the fear eating my guts. It's only a game you will say, but you're wrong. It's more than a game for people like me. You take all your feelings and you put them on the table and, if you do badly, it tears something out of you. Everything gets a bit colder and the brightest sunshine won't warm you up. You feel empty for days.

All around me, the rest of the City fans were boiling over with frustration.

'GET HIM OFF AND PUT HIS GRANNY ON!'

'I'VE SEEN BETTER FOOTBALLERS IN A DEEP FREEZE!'

Right on half-time, United scored. Nothing special, just a wild mix up after a corner, and BOOM! there was the ball in the back of our net.

'OOOOW!' City sighed.

'YAAAAAA!' United roared, arms in the air.

The half-time whistle sounded.

By now the sky was black with needles of hail slashing down past the pale floodlights that stared down on the miserable scene.

Me and Nosher headed for the fast food stall, where else? I looked up and saw our street, Barley Street, way across the valley, with the great brewery chimney next to it. Suddenly, I felt bad about leaving Suzie behind. I'd phone as soon as possible after the match, maybe.

Down in the sweaty crowds under the stand, I wasn't hungry but Nosher queued for yet another messy snack.

'They're going to take us to pieces in the second half!' I said.

'Don't give up, young 'un!' said a leathery old

fan. 'Just watch Joe. He can beat them on his own.'

Somebody must have told City to play it long to Joe in the second half. They were forever booting the ball towards him but the wind blew it through to the United keeper.

The minutes raced by. All this big kicking and the howling wind kept United back. The pitch got more and more like a birthday cake as now the snow came spinning down from the grey sky. The game was bogged down in midfield but United didn't care. They were winning.

In what seemed like no time, there were less than five minutes left.

'GET HIM OFF!'

'WHAT A LOAD OF RUBBISH!'

'GO ON, JOE. *DO* SOMETHING!'

The City fans were exploding again. The match was dead and gone even at one-nil.

'We've had it, you know!' Nosher was moaning. 'We haven't been in United's half for ten minutes! We haven't had one shot all game! It's hopeless! Let's go home now. We'll miss the bus queues!'

'No,' I said. 'There's still a chance. One goal and we're back in it.'

'Why? Have we got Superman as a sub? Forget it. The ref'll blow any second.'

'Watch Joe!' I said.

Nosher groaned and stuffed his face with another fistful of crisps.

'He's only one player! The rest of the team are terrible. Don't know why we come.'

Down there, far below in the icy wasteland, Joe prowled the pitch waiting for his chance.

The United fans started to whistle as the referee looked at his watch, but he waved play on. Finally, the City keeper got the ball and booted it mightily towards the United goal.

Up and up it went until it was lost in the blazing, snowy lights. A quick nudge from Joe, a slip by the sweeper and the giant striker was away.

'Go on, Joe!'

He was over the half-way line and heading for goal.

'Hit it, Joe!'

Twenty-five thousand of us were screaming. Joe was flying but someone was chasing. He was only thirty metres out but still he didn't shoot. On he went into the 'D' of the penalty area, over the line and – a leg came from nowhere to whip his feet away.

'PENALTY!'

The referee was pointing to the spot.

Joe crashed face down but, in a flash, leapt up angrily.

We all jeered, making donkey noises. 'EE-HAW! EE-HAW!'

Out came the red card and the United defender was gone But it didn't matter. Apart from the penalty, time was up.

Joe was the penalty ace. Now United would have the victory snatched from them. Up he got to place the ball ready for the kick.

Then I saw the danger. One minute, everything was perfect. The next, I saw the ref walking across the area, stiff as a penguin so he wouldn't fall over. I saw the shiny ball, slippery as soap. The floodlights gleamed on the ice between the patches of mud. The kick was not so easy after all.

Joe limped a little as he walked back. Still, he hadn't missed a penalty for two seasons!

We were all so still. The keeper bounced like a toy monkey on a spring. Fifty thousand held their breath. Nobody noticed the snow or felt the cold. Big Joe took a long, stomping run but, just before he got to the ball, I gripped the air-horn so tight that BAHHHHHHH! It roared out in the quiet stadium.

CHAPTER 4

Penalty!

Wup! Joe's mighty boot blasted the ball. The keeper had no chance with the shot as it blurred past him like a white cannonball.

'YEHHH!' The City fans rose for the goal. But the ball smashed madly into the bar and flew back over Joe's head almost to the half-way line.

'OOOAAAAAHH!' A terrible groan of pain came from the City fans. The referee blew for time and the United players punched the air.

'No! No! Noooo!' I shouted.

'He's missed it! He has,' groaned Nosher.

'I know, thickhead! I'm *here!*'

Then, I noticed something curious. Joe Jackson was still standing on the penalty spot. He didn't have his head in his hands like the other City players. He was staring up at the booing crowd behind the goal! Joe's face was harder than ever. Suddenly, he pointed violently first to his head then straight at me.

'I put him off, lost it for us! He's saying I'm mad!'

'Forget it!' said Nosher biting the head off a Mars bar. 'Let's go!'

'No, wait,' I said. Joe was still staring up.

'I bet you're glad you're not him!' muttered Nosher, still munching. 'If we get a penalty tomorrow in the cup semi, you'd better make a better job of it than that!' He laughed.

It was all right for Nosher to talk, he didn't have to take it, did he? He was our keeper. The game the day after, Adswood Celtic, was our top game to date but I couldn't think about it. All my thoughts were on that missed kick. The pain was terrible.

'Come on, let's get some chips,' said Nosher. 'At least we can't lose there!'

'I don't feel like it,' I said, hypnotized by that lonely figure down on the pitch.

'Look,' said Nosher, 'I'm off. Coming?'

'No,' I said.

'Suit yourself!' he grunted and trudged away. 'See you tomorrow!'

I headed for the wall behind the goal without even thanking Nosh for the ticket.

I had to talk to Joe. I had to say something. But when I got quite close to the goal, a steward stepped into my path and pointed to an exit.

'No, son. That way!'

It was over. The dream was over, ripped apart like the programmes on the floor of the empty stand. I raised a hand and shouted '*JOE!*' There was something in his face that really got to me. He gave a little wave and turned to make the long walk to the dressing room. He wasn't hunched or crumpled like the other City players had been.

'Oh, Joe,' I thought. 'Why did I have to put you off with that air-horn?'

Now it was time for me to hang up my dream for another week; time to live on the other side

of my head again and feel small.

The special buses had all gone. The quickest way to town was down the main road, but I'd be ambushed by United yobs full of power and glory, all psyched-up by the match.

Hmm! Better wait.

There's a supporters' centre attached to the ground, a place where no United fans go. I put my hand in my pocket and there was the crumpled tenner Dad had given me! And, as I headed for the building, I saw a big black car parked outside the private club the players have down there – JJJ1. Maybe I would get to speak to Joe after all?

But waiting for Joe was going to take time. I remembered the promise I'd made myself at half-time. I had to phone Suzie.

'Sean!' She sounded glad to hear my voice.

'What's happened?' I asked. 'I'm in the City Club waiting for Joe Jackson.'

'I don't know,' she said quietly, 'but there's *something* going on!'

'Like . . . ?'

'Like Mum got up before I bunked off to Gran's and she was so quiet.'

'*Quiet?*'

'Yes *and* she was really polite to Dad.'

'Polite to Dad? Has he won the lottery or something?'

'Don't joke, Steve. It's not funny. Anyway, she said, "It's all going to be sorted out soon and everyone will get what they want." What do you think *that* meant?' Suzie went on, 'Then she said something really weird to him. She said, "You going to Sean's match tomorrow?"'

'But she never said anything to me!'

'I know. And he said, "Yes. Why?" And she said, "Maybe I'll go." Why is she interested in football now? I just don't get it.'

'Me neither,' I said, my head buzzing. Mum was more interested in the greyhound results on Mars than my football. She'd buy me gear but interested? Never.

'Oh and by the way,' added Suzie. 'I took all your stuff for tomorrow's game to Gran's. Just in case you couldn't get in at home.'

'You genius! I'll see you there later. Where *is* Dad, by the way?'

'Don't know, when I phoned home the line was engaged.'

'I'll see you later then,' I said.

'How much later?' she asked sadly.

'Don't know.'

'Don't disappear!'

'Would I? I'm playing in the morning.'

'Don't be very late!' she said strongly.

The phone clicked down.

Six o'clock turned to seven and seven to

eight. The gleaming Jag stayed where it was. The tenner went down and down. I broke my promise to Suzie and let time drift by. Ten o'clock came; time to go to Gran's. The black Jag sat alone. No Joe. What a stupid waste of time and money!

CHAPTER 5

The crash

New Zealand Road is long, dark, steep and twisty. When I was a little kid, I didn't like it because it was so quiet and spooky but this particular Saturday I loved it because it had no United fans there.

But, all in all, I wasn't happy. I felt bad about Joe's penalty, bad about City losing, bad about everything at home. I had to lift myself somehow before the game tomorrow.

One or two cars came whizzing by, pinning me to the wall. Getting crippled in a car accident was all I needed. I had to get to Gran's in one piece, and play my match in the morning.

Then I had a shock. As I went down towards Vernon Park, a couple of long roads from Gran's, I heard a deep growling sound behind me. A powerful car was zipping down the zig-zag road from high above. Shrieking brakes told me that it was heading down the hill fast. Much too fast. I leapt off the road in a second.

Ahead was a sharp right-hand bend. One look at the approaching lights told me the car wasn't going to make it. It squirmed sideways like a rattlesnake as the driver struggled with the controls, but he had no chance on light snow at that speed!

SHAA! Brakes were on but not biting. It wasn't a car now, it was a sledge. WISH! It hissed by. CRASSSHH!

I looked up and it was gone! Somewhere I could still hear the deep rumble of the engine. But where was the car?

Down the road I ran. Wow! What a massive hole in the hedge! I followed the skid-marks over the bowling green and across the pitch and putt course, ending up in Vernon Park itself. The crabby old park keepers were going to have a fit when they saw what had happened. I ran towards the car.

The engine thundered on. The driver did not get out. Then the number plate 'JJJ1' leapt up at me. Joe's car!

Was he hurt? Was he . . . dead? I opened the door and he almost fell out.

'Got . . . got . . . get . . . ,' Joe held his head.

'You hurt, Joe?'

'No . . . no . . . got . . . ,' I could hardly make out what he was saying.

Suddenly my mind was in overdrive. The very next driver down New Zealand Road would phone the police. They would find Joe and he would be all over the papers – again. Joe was in a mess. On top of the penalty miss – he'd never be able to live it down. Maybe he'd go to court. There was nothing the papers liked better than to pull down a star when he was on the slide.

I dragged him over to the passenger seat and he flopped like a jellyfish. The car rumbled on. Lights were coming down the hill. I jumped into the driver's seat. What should I do? It was a monster, but it wasn't so different from Uncle Charlie's big Granada on the farm, was it? And the track used by park vehicles ran right past the back of Gran's, so I didn't have to go on any roads.

Easy, easy! HRUMMMMMMMMMMMM!!! HERUMMMMMMM!!!

The great beast knew its master wasn't driving. Ease it into first gear. KERCHUG! KERCHUG! The monster chugged slowly along, then turned into a bucking bronco. Then ZUP! Cut out!

Go on, you stupid machine!

HRUMM!!!! SHAA!!!! Away! And so was half the turf on the green.

I drove the car slowly up the dirt path, not daring to come out of first gear. I knew this road. I'd played down here since I was a little kid. Nobody ever came down here at night. I saw in the mirror that back on the road, car lights were shining on the hole in the hedge. Whoever it was must be wondering what had happened.

I tried not to panic and drove along very slowly. I shouldn't have been driving the car, but I felt like I owed Joe one and that was that. He was special, he was *our* Joe. He was the best we'd got.

Gran's house was five minutes down the track. And Gran. How would I get past Gran?

Just then, Joe spoke. 'Hey? Where are we?'

'Down the back of Vernon Park. Remember?

You ran through the hedge and carved up the bowling green.'

Joe was still rubbing his head.

'Where did you come from then?' he asked.

'I was walking down New Zealand Road. You crashed in front of me.'

'Ah, yes,' he said, staring at me.

Houses appeared ahead.

'Do you want to drive?' I asked.

'No,' he said. 'I don't think that would be a good idea.' His voice was fuzzy.

'I could phone for a taxi if you need to go to the hospital?'

'No taxi, no hospital,' said Joe, his voice still blurred.

Behind us, far behind, a siren was singing. The people who found the hole must have had a mobile phone and maybe called an ambulance. The police might be on the scene any minute. My mind was on fire. What could I do?

Behind Gran's house was a garage that she never locked. I opened the door, eased the Jaguar slowly in and turned off the engine.

'Where . . . where?' started Joe.

'My Gran lives here. She's used to people coming and going . . . I'll . . . say you're our team coach . . . that your car's broken down.'

Suddenly the whole weight of the world was on me. It wasn't half a mile from the Park but I felt like elephants had been rolling on me. I was worn out. Also, I'm not a good liar. Things were going to get awkward the second Gran opened the door.

Joe swayed along beside me. I knocked on the door, Gran came out and eyed Joe. But as soon as I started my story she raised an eyebrow.

'Coach, Sean? I wasn't born yesterday! I know who *this* is!'

'Mrs *Connor!* . . .' Joe started. He knew her!

The siren in the distance grew louder.

'Better come in, Joe,' said Gran looking in the direction of the noise.

'Thanks,' said Joe simply.

Gran looked at him hard. 'Still getting into trouble at your age?' she said sharply.

Big Joe seemed to shrink a bit. 'I'm really grateful . . . Mrs Connor!' he muttered.

'Come in and have a cup of tea,' was all Gran said.

All the while, I was dying to ask how she knew him. But something in her voice told me I couldn't ask her in front of Joe. Did she know he was the star striker for City? She was almost rude to him! And big Joe – he just took it, as if he was used to being told off by her!

Then Suzie appeared and we had an awkward cup of tea. Gran was angry that I'd driven Joe's car, but her voice softened as she said, 'At least *you* didn't leave *him* in trouble.' Joe looked embarrassed and uncomfortable. Soon he went upstairs to wash his face.

Immediately I faced her. 'How do you know

Joe?' I asked.

'It's a long story,' she replied slowly. I knew Gran. She wasn't going to talk. There was a long pause. Then she said, 'Ask your dad.'

'Where is Dad?' asked Suzie.

Gran shrugged. 'He said he'd come over this evening but your phone has been off the hook all afternoon.' She went on ominously, 'I hope Joe's gone before your dad gets here.'

'*Why?*' I asked emphatically.

She didn't answer.

Police, trouble at home. What next?

CHAPTER 6

More mysteries

Before Joe came back downstairs, Gran snapped, 'Time for bed you two!'

I was worn out *and* I was supposed to be playing football in the morning. I went upstairs wearily. Suzie wasn't happy either. 'Don't you think we've got *enough* problems without getting mixed up in other people's?' she said.

'But it's Joe!' I said. 'And people have got it in for him.'

'No,' she said, 'he's trouble! And now we've got his trouble.'

At midnight, I was dozing when a car drew up

outside. Police? I jumped up. It was Dad. I crept to the door and listened down the stairs.

Conversation buzzed quietly in the kitchen. There were only two voices, Gran's and Dad's.

'Wanted to check on the kids.' That was Dad.

I couldn't pick up what Gran said next but Dad replied, 'Joe Jackson! *Him* of all people!' Dad sounded amazed.

'Yes, but we don't want trouble.'

'Don't you remember what he did to me?'

'Well, yes . . .' said Gran, 'but think about the twins!'

There was a big silence.

My mind was whizzing. What *about* us? Come on, Dad! I thought. Talk about it! I couldn't wait to hear! But Dad said no more. Next thing there was a creak and a bump and Dad was lying in a sleeping bag on the carpet next to my bed.

I could feel my mind racing. What *had* Joe done to Dad? What was happening with Mum? Sirens echoed far away in the night, trains hummed across the great town viaduct, but finally I drifted away.

The next morning, I was first up with a

throbbing headache. And *this* was the day of the cup-tie!

I crept into the bathroom, splashed icy water on my face and made my way downstairs. I couldn't believe what had happened the night before. Joe. The crash. Driving to Gran's. It all seemed like a dream. Then I saw the huge figure stretched out asleep on the settee. Suddenly my mind jolted wide awake.

Gran met me on the way into the kitchen. She was coming out with two steaming cups of tea. 'One for you and one for the sleeping beauty,' she said nodding towards the settee. Dad's words from the night before were ringing my ears. What was their secret?

CHAPTER 7

You don't know anything about him

I coughed as I approached Joe. A gentle snoring was coming from the settee. Gran's idea of giving Joe tea was obvious – to wake him up so that he would go.

I put the cup on a small table by his side. 'Joe?'

'Uh?'

'JOE!'

I gave the big man a gentle shake on the shoulder.

'I've brought you some tea, Joe!' I said as I

drew the curtains.

Joe propped himself on one elbow and the street lights weren't kind to the grey in his hair or the great shadowy creases in his face.

'Very kind of you, son! Where are we?'

'Down near Vernon Park by the river.'

Joe put his hands to his face.

'I was driving . . .'

'You crashed on New Zealand Road in the snow. Made a right mess!'

Joe shook his head. 'Not *again!* The papers will finish me!'

'No they won't! Don't you remember?' I pointed out of the window. 'Your car's in Gran's garage.'

'I didn't hurt anyone . . .?' he started.

'No.'

Joe slumped in relief.

'You were very lucky,' I said seriously.

'Yes, I know,' said Joe quietly. There was a pause.

'It was my fault really,' I faltered.

'What was?' Now Joe looked puzzled.

'You getting fed up and driving so badly.'

Joe was shaking his head. 'How do you figure that one out?'

'It was me who blew the air-horn when you took the penalty.'

'Air-horn? What air-horn? We can't hear things like that down on the pitch!' The striker was grinning at the idea.

All of a sudden, I felt a huge relief. That was something I didn't need to worry about. I started to tell him about my own football, about the match that morning at Vernon Park.

'Sean!' Gran was calling.

'Got to go.' I was heading for the door.

'Don't worry, Sean. I won't hang around. And thanks, son. I won't forget what you did!'

Dad was at the kitchen table looking grey.

'Is *he* awake?' he said.

'Yes, I gave him a cup of tea,' I said. 'He was okay.'

'And . . .?'

'He's going soon.'

'Good!' Dad sighed.

'He's all right, you know.'

'You don't know anything about him.'

'Do you?' I wasn't happy at Dad's negative judgement.

'Went to school with him, didn't I?' he said. 'I've still got the marks!'

'He's not like that now.'

'You'll learn!'

I felt really irritated. Why was Dad so miserable about other people? No wonder Mum was tired of it all. There were steps in the hall, Dad looked tense but Suzie walked in, not Joe.

'Isn't Joe Jackson tall! He passed me going to

the bathroom. He fills the door! You'd better get four eggs on, Dad!'

'I don't see why . . .' he started.

Then the door opened again. Joe stood there, dark and wild with his curly hair flying away like witches' tresses.

'I suppose you'll want some breakfast?' said Dad.

'No thanks. I've been enough trouble to you, Frank. I'll be off.'

'Are you sure you're all right?' said Gran.

'I won't stay,' said Joe. 'You've been more than kind.'

He fiddled in his pockets for his car keys. I whipped them out of my jeans and handed them to him. He shook his head apologetically, then strode powerfully to the door. As he stepped outside, he turned to me and said again, 'I won't forget this.' Then he had gone.

'Maybe he *has* improved?' said Gran.

'No!' said Dad fiercely. There was a moment's silence.

'I've got to leave in half an hour,' I said. 'Kick off's at ten.'

Dad looked at me. 'I'll take you,' he said.

Then he was dialling home. Dialling and waiting. No reply. He hung up.

Gran said, 'Well?'

'Nothing,' he said. 'Nothing.'

Dad's call dragged my mind back to our house

on top of the windy hill. Think of the match, *the* match. But the unanswered phone thundered loudly in my ears. What's happened to Mum? What *is* going on?

CHAPTER 8

Cup-tie

'Boom! Boom!' There was a loud knocking at the door.

A big figure showed through the glass. Police? Had the skid marks on the golf course been traced back to Gran's? Had I been spotted?

A glance out of the window showed no patrol car. Phew!

When I opened up, Nosher rushed in with a red face and a torrent of words. 'Tried your house, Sean. No go, so I thought you'd be down here, seeing as how we're only playing round the corner. You haven't got a bit of toast have you, Mrs Connor? I'm starving!'

We all grinned.

'Ready for the game, Nosh?' asked Dad a few minutes later. 'All fuelled up now?'

I was starting to feel jumpy.

'Pity about Joe's penalty!' chattered Nosh.

'Shut up, Nosher!' I snapped. 'Can we go, Dad?'

'Nosher hasn't finished his loaf . . . I mean, slice yet,' said Gran.

We all laughed at her mistake, even Nosher. But he still finished his sixth slice and left with butter round his mouth like yellow lipstick.

Now it was time for football. Dad's old Mondeo took us to the bare park, where soapy ghosts of pollution floated across the hilly little pitch on the banks of the river. Only my team, Park Villa, played there.

Like City, Villa were not a great team. We had a few good players: Oggy Ogley in midfield, chunky Neil Miller and Sunil Kumar at the back, speedy Pete Silgram up front and Nosher keeping goal. But they relied a lot on me as captain and striker.

The dusty, concrete changing room was an ice box and the lads huddled and blew on their fingers as our coach, Jock Lindsay, gave us our instructions. 'We've got to *fight* like City did yesterday!' he said.

'Yeh,' agreed the lads.

'Pity about Joe's penalty,' somebody said.

There was an explosion in my head.

'I wish everybody would shut up about that penalty!' I snapped.

The changing room went quiet. 'Today is *our* game!' I went on.

YEH!!!

Then we were on the pitch. Adswood Celtic were big! And they too had their stars: tricky Lee Moston up front, speedy Lulu Lewis on the left and most of all, big Tom Parker who ran the team from the right midfield.

I could see the other team looking at me.

'Take out Connor and they're finished!' I heard one lad say.

I smiled. If they said that, they were afraid, just the way people feared Joe. Nobody wants to get a bad player off the pitch except his own team!

We had a bit of luck, won the toss and played down the hill in the first half.

I didn't hang around to be chopped down. I ran and ran and ran, making little dummies one way then the other like Joe, probing, always probing and finding space, just like he did.

Celtic stormed into the attack. It was their style. They left spaces at the back. Sunil saw his chance and, following a corner, made a break into midfield before chipping the ball over the last defender. The question was – would the hill and wind carry it on to the Celtic keeper before

I got to it?

Their keeper was as big as I am and I'm a big boy for my age. He came out fast. I charged in even faster and just got a toe to the ball before we ended up in a big heap in the goal area.

Penalty? Oh, no! Normally, I loved them, but after Joe's miss the day before I was anxious. But no. There was no penalty to take! The ref was pointing to the middle. In trying to bundle me over, the keeper had missed the ball altogether. Now it sat all alone in the back of the Adswood Celtic net. One-nil to Park. Yes!

However, the game changed. After the goal, I was double-marked and no matter how many zig-zag runs I made, I didn't get another shot.

Half-time: one-nil. Not enough. Now *we* were facing the big hill. Now Celtic had all the advantages.

Jock Lindsay shouted at us, 'After Sean's goal, they man-marked him. So, what did you do? Blasted it at him all the time. Think, lads, think! Now *we're* up against it, facing that slope.'

All this time, I had been watching the crowd. I didn't know why. I just had a funny feeling.

There was a gasp. Suddenly, Joe Jackson was there, towering over us. 'Do you mind if I say something?' said the big striker.

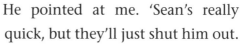

'Be my guest!' said Jock.

The boys hung on to Joe's words. 'The pitch slopes towards the river and sideways. The ball is going to end up with that big lad, Parker on their right midfield.'

He pointed at me. 'Sean's really quick, but they'll just shut him out. Why don't you have him marking *their* star kid out of it and see what *they* can do without *him*? That lad there, Oggy, would be okay up front and Sunil might be able to get in on the breaks too. If Celtic get frustrated they might lose shape, leave gaps.'

Off we went. I switched with Oggy, and the second half was on its way.

'Watch the Parker boy, hustle him, harass him. Give him a hard time,' said Joe.

As soon as the switch was made, you could see Adswood looking puzzled. What was I doing way back there in midfield?

In the first minute, I caught Tom Parker with two crunching tackles and after that his team were forced to leave him alone.

The second half ticked by. Celtic became more and more tensed up. The ball often ended out of play down the slope. The pitch was like an uneven pool table where the ball always heads for the same pocket. As everyone got tired, they all ended up in the same quarter of the field. Somehow, Nosher, his burgers, chips and toast managed to keep Adswood Celtic out until five minutes off the end. Then I noticed someone else watching us from the far side of the river. It was a tall, dark-haired woman in a leather jacket. Mum?

I was running down to the edge of the water to retrieve the ball for a throw-in. I looked, bent down for the ball, looked again and she was gone.

What did she want? She never came to watch me. My heart leapt. Maybe things weren't so bad, maybe things would work out after all? My concentration lapsed and Tom slipped away from me.

'Mark your man, Sean!' Dad shouted, but it was too late. The other boy was away, rocketing the ball past Nosher who flopped about like a great whale in the mud.

GOAL!

Parker punched the air. I could see he was thinking: now for the winner.

The sky darkened and rain started to pour. The ref looked at his watch. Then it happened. Nosh made a great catch and followed it by doing the strangest thing. He rushed up the field with the ball.

'Nosher's gone mad!' people shouted.

Attackers backed right off expecting a big kick. Then they were laughing. Nosher stormed on, red-faced, towards the half-way line.

'You can't stop me!' yelled Nosh. Soon, he was actually on the half-way line! Somebody once said, 'All goalkeepers are mad.' Here was the living proof of it!

Suddenly, Celtic woke up, saw the chance of catching him out of his area. I knew that Nosher would hoof it hard and long and started to sprint. I ran, Oggy ran and Sunil ran. If we lost the ball, there was an open goal at our end.

WHAP!

And indeed, Nosher did boot the ball really high towards the other goal. I led the chase, racing to get under the towering kick. Pete and the others were closing fast too. A central defender went to head it but it skimmed past him like a cake of soap. Now it was a chase between their keeper and the hunting pack. The slope slowed the ball. I dummied left and went right, touched the ball past the goalie and – his hand came out and I was down.

PENALTY!

Off went the keeper. In went their sweeper as a substitute goal-keeper.

'How much longer, ref?' called Jock Lindsay.

'Half a minute from the kick,' was the reply.

Substitute keeper. How could I fail? But then Joe Jackson's miss was fifty metres high in my mind. If Joe could miss, anyone could.

'I don't want this one,' I shouted.

'Go on. Sean!' The team pleaded.

'Chicken!' sneered the keeper.

'Cut it out, son!' snapped the ref.

I took a long run. 'I'm going to miss it. It's fate. It's yesterday all over again,' I thought.

WHAP!

It was the biggest mis-kick of all time. The ball spun madly like a top towards the middle of the goal, but the keeper dived flat-out to his right. On and on the ball bobbled as the lad struggled to get up from the frosty mud. The ball hit him on the studs of his left boot and bounced slowly into the left hand corner of the net.

YAAA!! GOAL!

The kick-off was taken. Lee Moston tried a

shot from a mad distance and missed. Then the whistle went and we'd won! This isn't real, I thought. It worked out just right.

That was the worst penalty ever taken. I was so very lucky. Me, lucky! Wow! I'd spent all morning gearing up my mind for another blow and we'd won! Somehow it was more shocking than losing.

'Someone up there likes you, son! Put in a word for me!' laughed Joe. 'I'll be off now! Well done, lads!'

'We're practising at the City Dome on

Wednesday,' I shouted.

Joe turned. 'I'll be there,' he said.

Joe was interested in me, fantastic!

Suzie hugged me and Nosher.

'Great!' she said. 'Just great!'

'That was fantastic, Sean!' Dad seemed almost in tears. I could see him looking at me with new eyes. It was as if he'd never really seen me. Then he stared at Joe, who was walking away. It was really odd.

'Great penalty!' said Nosher. 'Anyone got any eats? I'm starving.'

Suzie produced a Mars bar and he stuffed it into his mouth.

'So it's Cale Green in the final at City's ground on Saturday!' shouted Jock.

Cale Green! OOOO! They had Tony Street!

That's something to worry about tomorrow! I thought. Let's enjoy today!

Jock fished out one of those pump-action flasks that hold gallons of hot tea and all the lads slurped it down like champagne.

Then there was the red-hot shower fizzing all over us. Was there anything closer to heaven on an icy day after a great win than a hot drink and a sizzling shower? This was our Wembley! This was paradise!

WE'RE THE PARK! BAM-BAM-BAM! The stamps and cheers shook the walls. Adswood Celtic crawled out quietly. Their world was just cold feet and aching bones. Whoever ached when they won? Life was looking up. And then I thought about the woman on the other side of the river. If it *was* Mum, what was she doing there?

CHAPTER 9

A nasty surprise

I got changed quickly and went outside. I left Suzie getting warm in Dad's car and wandered down to the pitch again. On the far side of the river, a black Jaguar was rumbling up the road – Joe? Then I saw that there was a woman watching it move away – Mum?

'Mum!' I shouted. She turned, put her hand to her mouth, then vanished behind the trees.

Mum talking to Joe Jackson? Was *that* why my dad didn't like him?

Ten minutes later, we were driving through town as light snow feathered down from the steely sky. Suzie stared ahead. Up the hill we went, past Gran's, along the ridge towards the giant chimney with *Grundy's Beer* on it. Now the snow was making spider's webs in the trees along Love Lane and, finally, there it was, Barley Street with the city stretched out behind it all misty and delicate like a Chinese painting.

Dad stopped the car in front of our house. Nobody spoke. The silence was very loud. I was first through the door.

'Hey!' I said. 'We've been burgled!'

The lounge was empty, no carpet, no three-piece suite, no TV, no stereo.

I raced into my room. It was exactly as I'd left it. There was nothing missing. I ran to Mum's wardrobe and opened it. Her clothes were gone.

'Sean?' Suzie called.

'It's Mum,' I said. 'She's gone!'

Dad sat at the kitchen table holding a letter.

'I'll have . . . to go out . . . I've got to go . . .' he muttered.

'Now?' My voice was buzzing. 'And leave us again?'

I looked at Suzie but she was shaking her head at me.

Dad staggered on. 'You see . . . I've got to . . . think . . .'

'Why can't you think here?' I almost shouted.

He moved for the door. I tried to cut him off but it was no good. Without another word, he went past and out. The front door slammed, echoing around the empty house.

'I don't believe it!' I snorted and went to the window. 'Hey, he hasn't taken the car!'

'Of course he hasn't. He's gone to the Three

Stars. Don't worry about him. He'll be back.'

'Where is Mum, Suzie? What's happened?'

'She's gone, just gone,' she said putting her arms round me.

'Do you think she'll come back?' I hugged her with my head over her shoulder.

'I don't know,' she said with a dull voice. 'Why would she?'

'What have we done? Why did it happen to us?'

Suzie looked me in the eye. 'Sean, it's not us! Today was just the day it happened. They were on different planets.'

Suddenly, the day caught up with me and I flopped down next to Suzie. We lay and dozed in front of the fire, worn out by it all.

When I woke up, the house was very peaceful. Everything felt unreal. Life was like a film. I could hear my voice saying the lines. Nine o'clock passed. Then ten. Then eleven.

The door clattered and in came Dad on wobbly legs with a bag full of Chinese take-away. We were bursting with questions that seemed impossible to ask.

'Cup of tea, Dad?' said Suzie as if it was just an ordinary day.

'No . . . er . . . bed . . .' he said foggily and bumped upstairs, leaving the hot greasy bag behind.

In five minutes, the food was gone. In ten, I was in bed exhausted yet unable to sleep. Suppose it was something *I'd* done that tipped Mum over the edge? Suzie was perfect. It had to be me. I wracked my brains to think of what it could have been that made her snap.

The phone rang out, deafening in the silence, and, in a flash, I was downstairs answering it.

'Hello,' I said. 'Mum? Mum? *Please say something, Mum!'*

But there was no reply.

CHAPTER 10

Trouble

In the morning, I was up really early.

'Where's Dad?'

'In bed,' Suzie sighed. 'Leave him alone. We are going to school,' she went on. 'Both of us.'

'*I* wasn't going to bunk off!' I said.

'Hmm!' she said, just like Gran.

Just then, the local paper clattered through the letter box. I went to get it. Suddenly I went cold.

The headlines screamed out at me:

'JOE TO GO?'

Joe was facing the axe. That missed penalty

had been enough to set them all on his back. He was too expensive, too old. But maybe he could fight back? I couldn't stop thinking about it. At eight-thirty, I slung a bag over my shoulder and headed for the door.

'Hey! Wait for me!' Suzie's voice floated out as the door slammed.

School. Ten stops down the line on the Cityrail tram – Seaham Central High School, glass door, spiked fences.

I stood in the yard in the middle of the whirling crowd.

'Villa! Villa!'

Nosher stood eating oven chips from the breakfast canteen as the rest of the team kept the chant going.

Then Tony Street came by, laughing. He was small and broad and dark. 'Good luck in the final, lads,' he said and went off grinning.

'Hey,' said Oggy Ogley, 'we're playing Cale Green in the final. That's *his* team.'

'I know,' said Nosher suddenly forgetting how to chant. 'And he plays for England Boys!'

'*There* you are!' a stroppy voice cut in. It was

Suzie. 'Don't you walk off and leave me like that when I've made your breakfast!'

'I'll walk off anytime I want!' I snapped.

'Suit yourself!' she said and stalked off. 'You do that!'

'Why did she make your breakfast and not your mum or dad?' nosed Nosher.

'Shut up!' I stormed and elbowed my way through the crowd.

In class, I looked across to where Suzie was sitting. Normally, she would be bouncing around talking about what she'd done at the weekend, but today she sat quietly as her friends rattled on about London.

The gap across the classroom felt very wide. I could not believe what was happening. I could not believe the speed with which cracks were appearing in my life.

The week ahead stood before me like a steep hill and behind that the next week towered up, another grey peak. The year ahead was like Everest.

'Sean?'

'Oh, er, yes, Miss!'

Miss Taylor, my form teacher, asked, 'Good game on Sunday?'

'Yes, Miss.'

'In the final now?'

'Yes, Miss.'

'Good lad, but don't dream about it all day!'

'No, Miss!'

The bell went. Suzie flagged me down.

'Yeh?'

'Say nothing about what's going on at home, *understand?*' she snapped.

'Why?'

'Because I'm *not* taking any of that patronizing "single-parent" rubbish off anybody. You understand?'

'Err . . .'

'Yes?' she insisted.

'All right.'

I'd never seen her so strong. Everything seemed like hard work to me but she seemed to be coping well. However, what happened in science told me differently.

When she showed Mr Bigland her book, he went mad.

'Suzie, I don't know what to say. It's just so . . . poor . . . not up to your usual standard at all . . .' he started.

'OO! Suzie!' some of the lads jeered.

'Just shut it!' she snapped.

'OOO!' Even more.

Russell May, the class lout was loving it. 'Oh, Miss Swotty's got it wrong.'

'Shut it, I said!'

'Suzie! Suzie! *Calm down!*' Kind Mr Bigland was amazed.

'I'll do it again tonight,' she said, glaring at

Russell. 'I had . . . a headache, sir. That's all.'

Old Bigland still looked confused. 'A headache? Why didn't you say?'

'I just hate making excuses, sir!'

Soon it was afternoon. Art drifted past me without any problems. Then I found myself in the P.E. corridor.

Nick Doogan, the ginger P.E. teacher, posed like the Lion King on his concrete step to make himself look taller.

My mind turned to ice. I liked P.E., but now I was in a mess. For the first time since Junior school, there I was without any kit. I looked into my bag as if it had betrayed me. I felt a complete fool. Doogan went mad when you forgot your kit.

'All those mugs without any kit, *out here!*' he yelled.

I trailed out to join the usual crew of drop-outs led by Russell.

Doogan's eyes popped at the sight of me.

'Notes!' said the teacher grimly. 'And they'd better be good!'

Russell handed his mum's note in. You could

smell the scent all down the line.

'What's this, "athlete's foot"?'

'Yes, sir.'

Doogan handed the note back without smiling. 'All you need now is an athlete's body to go with it.'

I was at the end of the line.

'Sean?' he said astounded. 'Injured?'

'Sir,' I whispered.

'Well? Are you injured or not?'

I could feel my face going red.

'Can I talk to you? Privately?'

'Wait here.'

I looked at the floor. The teacher pointed to the able-bodied members of the class. 'You lot – in, changed and silent – in two minutes.'

Then it was the turn of the drop-outs.

'You lot – plastic bags – litter picking!'

'What about him?' Russell was pointing at me.

'Russell,' said Doogan with a sigh, 'do you want to play football in a netball skirt?'

Suddenly they had all gone.

'Well?' the P.E. man was focussing on me.

I heard Suzie's voice in my head. 'Don't tell anyone!'

I bit my lip. I didn't want to say anything, but I didn't want earache off Doogan either. Things started to go wobbly, misty.

Suddenly Doogan's face was there, closer.

'Trouble?'

I nodded.

I couldn't see his face any more.

'Mum's gone.'

Doogan just looked at me. Then he patted me

on the shoulder.

'Got a spare kit in here, Sean, and boots. Size seven aren't you?'

The kit was handed over.

'Thanks, sir!'

'Next time, full kit, whatever, okay?'

I went off to get changed but as I looked up I saw Suzie watching from the girls' gallery above and shaking her head angrily. *Now everybody will know. Everybody. Pathetic.* I could read her expression.

CHAPTER 11

Surprises

The games lesson was terrible, but I wasn't the only one off-form. Even Tony Street seemed to have two left feet that day.

Doogan was not happy. We spent almost all the time working on skills.

By the end, I felt exhausted. Life, even football, felt dead.

I couldn't wait for Doogan to set us free. Finally, he pointed to the door. 'Open the cage!' he said and we filed out.

Suzie was waiting for me at the gate with a face like stone.

'Don't say anything,' I said.

'Why not?'

'Because whatever you were going to say, I already know! Believe me, I know because I've said it to myself.'

She kept quiet.

We toiled down the road on to the tram. It rumbled across the gloomy city, up towards the brewery chimney. Finally, we stepped down. Not one word had been spoken all the way. Up above was the cobbled hill and Barley Street.

When we got home, the house was empty. No Dad, no message, nothing.

That evening, he was due on night shift at the hospital where he worked as a porter. He should have been at home. A cold feeling went through me. Suzie got her books out on the kitchen table.

I was thinking of ringing Gran, but the thought of Suzie's reaction put me off. So I slipped upstairs and checked Dad's bedroom. His clothes were still there. He hadn't left us too.

I turned on my video and slotted in 'Joe Jackson's 50 Greatest Goals'. Some of them were from years back – headers, volleys, chips, penalties, the lot. After half an hour of this I looked up at the giant poster of him on the wall and saw my reflection in the mirror next to it:

similar dark, curly hair, similar high cheek-bones. I smiled. I was glad I looked a bit like him and, suddenly, the thought of the football final surged through my body and life didn't seem so bad after all.

I heard the phone ring. 'Where *are you?*' Suzie's voice was sharp. 'You are doing *what?* You *should* be here. How do you think we felt when the house was empty? See you too.' She slammed the phone down.

'What was that all about?' I asked.

'Dad was only out buying football kit, that's all!'

'What's he trying to do, compete with Joe?' As soon as I'd said it I realized that it might be true.

'Why would he want to do that?' asked Suzie.

'No idea,' I said, keeping my thoughts to myself.

*   *   *

When I got back home from school on Tuesday, I had a surprise. There was a shiny black hold-all by the settee and I could hear someone bumping around upstairs.

'Dad?' I called.

Dad came downstairs into the lounge and I just stared.

'Well, what do you think?' Dad said.

He was wearing an all-blue football kit.

'Dad!' was all I managed.

'Joe Jackson isn't the only footballer in the world, you know. I was quite good and played until I was about twenty but . . .'

'What?'

'Nothing. What do you reckon? I'm playing five-a-side for the Three Stars tonight at the Dome. You coming?'

Suzie was tied up with dancing in the Christmas Show at school.

'Hey, yeh, great!' I laughed. Dad playing football! Wow! Things were starting to change.

Just then, Suzie phoned. She'd be spending the night at Gran's. There was no rush for Dad and me to get home.

Roll on, seven o'clock. Roll on football.

*   *   *

The massive City Dome was crawling with people. Twenty-four pub teams and their supporters plus all the people playing a dozen other sports.

We watched from the gallery. The Three Stars were due to play in Group One and Dad had changed already. I saw the other team, looking like oven-ready turkeys. Beer and football didn't seem to go together. I was glad to see Dad in action but a bit anxious. Could he play? Would it be another failure? Something else never to be mentioned again?

Then the game got underway. The pitch was surrounded by a net so the ball never went out of play. The teams ran around like maniacs and it was more like watching a pinball machine than a football game. It was hard to tell if Dad was any better than the others. He only ever touched the ball for millionths of a second. All the heavyweights filled the pitch. It was like playing in a telephone box.

Then, towards the end of the fifteen minutes, a strange thing happened. The other team slowed down and there was space. The ball rolled towards Dad and he swerved right then went left. The court was clear ahead. He thundered the ball into the bottom left-hand corner.

'YEHHH!!!' I roared.

'Great goal!' boomed a voice in my ear. 'He learned *that* trick from me!'

Joe towered above me.

'From *you*, Joe?'

'Oh, yes. We used to play together for Moss Side before United signed me.' Joe smiled. It was very strange. The evening papers had said that Joe's future was still 'under consideration'. Everything seemed to have gone wrong for him and yet he was smiling.

'What was Dad like?' I was fascinated at the idea of them being team-mates.

'Frank? He could play all right. But things went wrong for him.'

'Like what?'

My mind was really buzzing.

'Well . . .'

Heavy breathing made me turn and there was Dad, sweating like a washed tomato but looking happier than I'd seen him for months.

'Great goal,' said Joe.

'One of your moves,' admitted Dad. 'I've only got three tricks. You've got a hundred,' he added sharply.

Joe gave him a careful look and seemed awkward.

'Good luck with the rest of the games,' he said and was gone, calling, 'See you tomorrow at the practice, Sean!' as he went.

'That was great, Dad. Get you a drink?'

'Thanks, son,' he said. 'Better make it a cola.'

The rest period of ten minutes passed quickly. Soon they were on the move again but slower. If it hadn't been for Dad, the Three Stars would have been slaughtered. He pulled the same trick as before. He dipped his shoulder left and went right. Wham! Another!

However, he couldn't be everywhere. Three goals rained in at the other end. Then it was over. The pub team's captain came up to Dad grinning. 'You're a quiet one! Not telling us you could play like that!'

'Great goal, Dad!' I said. 'Joe would have been pleased with that.'

'You like Joe, don't you?' he said quietly.

I nodded.

The Three Stars hadn't won, but I didn't care. We were in a good mood and we had the best evening we'd had for months.

CHAPTER 12

Plans

The next day Dad took me to the practice and at seven o'clock, we were up at the City Dome with the whole squad. Tony Street and Saturday's final loomed ahead of us. There was no sign of Joe.

'Thought you said Joe was coming?' sneered Wayne, the sub.

'He said he'd be here, so he *will!*' I said.

Jock Lindsay did not have much imagination and, after jogging around, we played five-a-side as usual.

'Look who's up there,' said Nosh.

I looked up and saw a chunky, dark-haired figure on the balcony. Tony Street. Watching, thinking and planning. I  raised a hand and Tony clapped silently before turning his thumb down. See you, Saturday, pal!

I thought. Make my day!

Then Dad suggested practising beating the last defender and shooting. I was on fire. When I was the last man, nobody but Pete got a shot in.

When I attacked, the ball screamed past Nosher again and again.

'There's Joe!' said Sunil suddenly, when we had stopped for a breather. Joe was talking to a man who nodded as Joe spoke and made twisting and turning movements with his hands.

'He's talking about you, Sean,' said Pete. 'That's how you play, twisting and turning and wrong-footing people with dummies.'

After our session we changed and gathered in the cafe on the gallery as usual. I noticed that Dad was missing.

'Hey, look, Sean! Your dad's talking to Joe Jackson!' Pete was looking down into the main hall. The two men stood in a distant corner arguing.

'They must be discussing tactics for Saturday,' said Nosher turning back towards his food. I knew that this wasn't true. Dad's head was bobbing and ducking. His hand was jabbing towards Joe. Joe was looking at the floor as he listened. Then as he spoke, he shook his head and he held up his hands in an innocent gesture.

Finally, Joe pointed to the cafe. Dad looked up and saw me. Suddenly his posture changed and he held his hand out for Joe to shake. I wasn't fooled. The two men went their different ways: Dad came to me. Joe went to the counter to be swamped by kids after his autograph.

'Got to get off soon,' said Dad briskly. 'Got to pick up Suzie.'

'She's staying at Gran's,' I reminded him.

'Oh, aye, anyway, best get home fairly soon. You'll have your homework to do.' Since when had he cared about my homework?

We set off for home but, when we got to the car park, I gripped Dad's arm. 'Hang on, Dad. I've forgotten to tell Nosher something.'

'Be quick then.' Dad strode on in the frosty night.

I flew but not to Nosher. Joe stood alone in the bar, looking thoughtful.

'Hi, Sean!'

'I've got to talk to you.'

'About Saturday?'

'No, Joe, about everything.'

Joe gave me a quick look.

'Here? Now?'

'No, give me your number. I'll phone you tomorrow night.'

'No,' said Joe, 'I'll phone you on Friday.'

'Promise. It's very important to me.'

'I know. Me too,' said Joe, his dark face

creasing with tension. He paused. 'A United scout was watching you tonight. He'll be there on Saturday, too.'

On the way home, my mind was buzzing. United! After *me?*

'Chinese or Indian, then?' Dad's voice brought me back to reality.

'Chinese,' I answered automatically.

Soon, we were home. As I ate the take-away, the world seemed to slow and my nose got dangerously close to the plate. Finally I flopped down on to the carpet in front of the gas fire and felt Dad cover me over with a duvet.

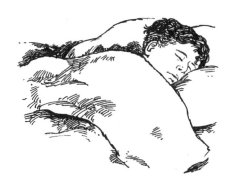

CHAPTER 13

Friday

Thursday and Friday were endless. It was the most important week of my life. Nothing seemed to have changed for years. Now it had all exploded and how would things end up?

I met Suzie in the yard on Thursday morning and told her about Dad's football. 'You should have seen him play! And *United* are watching me on Saturday!' I said.

'That's great!' she said looking happy for me.

'How's the show?' I asked.

'Great, just great!' she smiled. I could see she was still floating from the rehearsal the night before. Our form teacher had said she could be a professional dancer with the right training. I was thrilled, but horrified at the responsibility on my shoulders. What was I going to find out on Friday night? One wrong word could send her spiralling down too.

Thursday dragged by, but thoughts of the final got me through it. Friday lasted a fortnight, or so it seemed. I struggled with Maths, hacked my way through French, designed a cup for a blind person in Tech and splattered through Art. I felt impatient, counting the moments to Joe's call and the Saturday match. My confusing life might make sense, my football future could be bright. But I was like a climber who had only to make one slip to go crashing down into a terrible darkness. I could almost feel the drop beneath my feet, but there was no turning back.

Dad had tea with me, then went off to hospital for his late shift. Old Mrs Thomas from next door came in to see I was okay.

I lay by the fire with the phone by the scatter cushion, ready, waiting.

Eight o'clock came, no call.

BEEP-BEEP! My hand whipped out like lightning. This was *it*.

'Sean,' Suzie's strong voice echoed down the phone, 'I'm sleeping over at Deb's tonight, okay?'

'Okay,' I said, disappointed. 'See you tomorrow.'

'Okay,' she said and was gone.

I dozed in the warmth of the fire. Soon my mind drifted to Saturday, to City's ground. Wes had hit a perfect through ball. I had only the keeper to beat, dummy right, go left and . . .

BEEP-BEEP! BEEP-BEEP!

'Hi, it's me, Nosher! Guess what? I've got a copy of Striker 2001. Want to come and play me?'

Nosher always had the latest everything. All the time the keeper was talking I wondered if Joe was phoning.

'Sorry, Nosh. Got to stay in. I'm waiting for someone to phone.'

'Is it Karen Mackie?'

'No, it is *not* Karen,' I snapped.

'D'you want to come and play computer

games tomorrow night?' Nosh went on.

'I've got to go,' I said sharply.

'Don't you want to talk?' Nosher sounded hurt.

'I would if I wasn't waiting for Joe Jackson to phone me.'

'Wow! JOE JACKSON! What does he want?'

'It's to do with Saturday,' I lied.

'See you tomorrow then.'

Nosher clicked off. I put my head on the cushions. The phone lay silent.

I was back in the park taking the penalty again, but this time I smashed it up into the bar just the way Joe did . . . BOOOM! The noise it made was terrific.

BANG! BANG! BANG!

The noise went on and on. Then suddenly, I realized that the noise was not coming from the twanging crossbar in my dream, but the front door. I leapt up. It was Joe!

'What . . .?' I gasped.

'You wanted to talk to me,' said the giant footballer looking serious and grimmer than usual. 'Well, here I am.'

We went through to the back room.

'Phew! Cosy!' Joe said as he sat down by the gas fire. I was about to turn the light on but Joe said, 'No, leave it like this. It's better like this.'

I leaned against the scatter cushions and looked up at Joe's sad face. 'Do you want a cup of tea?' I asked.

'Yes, that'd be great.' Joe's voice was low and soft. It was an odd conversation. Neither of us quite knew how to start talking. Both of us were treading very carefully.

'You ready for tomorrow?' Joe shouted through as the kettle boiled.

'Yeh,' I called. I could see Joe through the crack of the door, staring into space. When I reappeared with a giant mug of tea for us both, Joe looked at me very carefully. The fire cast dark shadows across his great leathery face.

He hesitated. 'This has been a great week.'

What a weird thing to say! I thought. He missed an important penalty, nearly killed himself and City probably don't want him any more and he says it's been a great week!

But it was clear that he had something difficult to say. All of a sudden, he seemed to make up his mind and he went on, 'It's been good to see you and Suzie . . . But I've got something to tell you. When I've told you, perhaps you won't want to know me any more.'

I shivered, wondering what was coming.

Joe looked away as he spoke. 'There was a time when me and your dad were best friends, playing football together, drinking together and having a good time.

'Frank was the sensible one. I was the wild
one. I played for England Under-23s, was a pin-
up and all that stuff. I just couldn't get enough
of it, after the children's home where I got
treated like something the cat brought in. Then
she appeared on the scene and it was all
different.'

'Mum?'

'She went out with Frank at first but I was the
one with the flash car, wasn't I? Your dad didn't
make the grade as a footballer.'

'And . . . ?' I asked.

'Well, I started being all respectable when I met her. I was trying to impress her to get her to go out with me. Trying to break them up.'

'So?'

'Well, it worked . . . I married your mum.'

'YOU? You married Mum?' I could hardly speak, my voice sounded all choked and strange.

'Yes,' he said sadly, 'I was twenty-one and I thought I knew it all. But I messed up. The papers were full of stories of the cars I crashed, the bars I went to. Then your mum divorced me and I went off to play for a club in America. Your dad married her right away.'

My head was reeling from the shock. My mum married to Joe Jackson! I couldn't quite take it in. All sorts of thoughts flashed through my mind. No wonder Dad didn't like him! No wonder he hated it when I praised the City striker. It must have reminded him how Joe had won at every turn. There was a long silence. Joe was not looking at me.

Then I said, 'Why did you talk to Mum the other day?'

I couldn't help it – I sounded almost as if I was accusing him.

'Maybe you can't believe this –' Joe was speaking carefully, as if it hurt him, '– but I hadn't seen her for years. Then I saw her in the park last Sunday. She was watching you. She wanted to know if you were any good.' Joe forced out the words. 'She asked me what I thought. She cares about you, you know.'

Mum wanted to know if I was any good at football! My mind was whirling. I felt as if I was in the middle of a storm and yet I couldn't speak, I couldn't even look at the big footballer.

Joe stood staring into the fire. Then he stepped forward to look at himself in the mirror. Great shadows stretched up his face. 'Not a pretty sight, eh? Outside or in.'

I stood alongside him, a smaller shadow.

'Joe,' I asked at last, 'are you my real dad?'

Joe turned slowly and held me by the shoulders.

'Don't ask me that. Not now.' He turned. 'Better go,' he said.

There was a short silence and then I asked, 'Will you come to watch me in the morning?'

Joe turned in surprise. 'You still want me to?'

I saw the sadness in his eyes and nodded.

Then he was gone.

CHAPTER 14

Starting again

After Joe left, I lay in the darkness and thought hard and long. This talk with Joe was supposed to answer so many questions. It seemed to have raised even more. I couldn't take it all in. Joe didn't hate Dad, that was clear. But then, Dad had good reason to hate him. Would Mum come and see us again? What was going to happen?

Then I thought, hang on! It's the final tomorrow. All the bad ripples from that time so long ago have to stop somewhere. Someone has to start again. That someone could be me.

Mum did care about us. But she was gone. She

wasn't just testing Dad out. The furniture had gone with her. Suzie had been brilliant. She'd seen it coming and bounced right back. Dad had started to change and Gran was helping us too. Tomorrow was the start of *my* future.

United were watching me. This game was so important.

I carefully prepared my kit for the game. I folded the blue and white Villa gear and put it in my hold-all, oiled my soft boots yet again and put them in a plastic bag. And, as I was carrying out my careful ritual, I was thinking about the final, about taking the ball off Tony Street with a crunching tackle.

As I drifted off to sleep, I saw Tony smiling, giving me the thumbs down and saying, 'Good luck for the final, lads!'

'You can do it, Sean!' I said to myself.

CHAPTER 15

All or nothing

A clumping door woke me. I opened one eye. The sky was dark, the wind sang in the wires and my clock said 6.37. It was three hours and fifty-three minutes to kick off. I turned my light on, there was no time to sleep now.

I put on my headphones, flicked on my CD player and thought about the game, about something we had discussed based on our success with Tom Parker. I had to man-mark Tony in midfield. Oggy would cover behind me. Then there were four in line at the back. Wes Thompson, Sunil Kumar, Neil Miller and Vic

Long. Sometimes, not often, we'd be able to hit Cale Green on the break, switch from defence to attack quickly. Then, I would go forward to support Pete Silgram leaving Oggy behind to mark Tony Street. At least, that was the theory. However, although I was needed to stop Tony, I was also needed up front as we only had one other striker. Problem: I couldn't be in both places at the same time.

Eight o'clock. Dad brought me my pre-match breakfast: sweet tea, toast and honey.

'Nervous?' Dad asked.

'A bit.'

'You can do it. I know it.'

'If we can just start well, we might have a chance. Break their rhythm early. They've played us before you know.'

'And?'

'They won five-nil. I didn't play. It was that friendly in September when I was ill. They were two up in two minutes.'

'Tony?'

'Who else?' I said. 'But *if* we can stop them passing to him, it might get interesting. He likes the ball at his feet. He'll kill us if he is given any space, but he doesn't like running around a lot, chasing. If he has to cover back we might get a few breaks. He can't stop *me*. But can I stop *him?*'

I stood at the window and looked across the valley towards the ground.

'We'll set off at half-past nine?' said Dad.

'Okay, Dad.'

As usual, I checked my gear once again. Blue shirt, white shorts, blue socks, shin guards, blue velcro ties for my socks. Then the boots. I stroked the soft leather, slipped them on to my feet, sat on the bed and played the game in my head.

Dummy right, go left, one, two, BAM! Flick over the top, one bounce and BAM! Then a penalty. Left shoulder down as if to pull it to the keeper's right then WHAP! Sidefoot it into the other corner. Yes, YES!

Then there was a knock on my door. Suzie came in.

'Ready?'

'Guess so,' I said, packing my stuff yet again.

'Coming to the show tonight?'

'Just try and stop me!'

She looked pleased as she slipped out.

I was starting to feel twitchy. The clock was racing on. I looked at the big picture of Joe on the wall.

'Give me a bit of your magic today, Joe!'

The drive to the ground was quiet. I continued to think about scoring. We followed our usual bus route, down the town hill, across the city and along the river.

And then we were there. I was surprised at how many cars were parked outside. The final was normally played on City's training ground. Today was special and we had the main stadium. Today, there were a lot of people interested in the game, not just relatives. And they hadn't all come to watch me!

At once, I spotted Joe laughing with Sunil. Sunil smiled all the time. Others looked more nervous. Nosher wasn't even eating.

'Look at all these people. There must be two or three hundred here!' said Suzie.

'It's the final,' I said. 'It's what everyone's been waiting for.'

Tony grinned across at me and raised an arm. I nodded but wasn't in a smiley mood. I saw a flicker of worry in his eyes. Good!

Soon all the waiting and hoping were done. Soon we were out there in the great stadium, ready to begin.

I took Oggy to one side.

'If I go up you *must* mark Tony, otherwise we're *dead*.'

Oggy nodded. He, too, was pale.

'Stay tight on him, *tight*.'

Oggy nodded again. He's the youngest in the team and I could see he was nervous.

Just before the kick-off there was a wave from the touch line. Mum! Joe was right. She'd come to cheer me on!

The game began in the worse possible way. At the whistle, Tony ran hard down the middle. Ranjeet, Cale Green's big striker held the ball up then hit it hard and low at the star. I was up close, but Tony nicked it past me and won a metre on the turn. Oggy was miles away, after all

I'd said. Sunil left his own man to cover across. I stormed after the star, but Tony was picking which corner to put it in. Bam! Top right. Ten seconds played! One-nil!

'Oggy! Where were you?' My face burned. So much for the plan! The cheers for Tony were swirling round in my head. I was dizzy with shock and sick with disappointment. Another dream was melting like ice-cream in the sun. Come on, Sean! Come on! But the pain of going behind really hurt.

Soon, Cale Green had the ball again. Sam, their big, red-headed centre back stormed through the midfield. He was looking for Tony again but this time, I was ready for him. Ranjeet ran on past the last line of defenders. Sam chipped the ball over them. Off side. At least that bit of our plan worked. Keep a tight line at the back.

'Well done lads!' shouted Jock, our coach.

When Tony went wide on the right, I followed. When Tony went wide on the left, I was there too. At times we bumped elbows. At times, Tony tried to make a run and crashed into me or tripped over my long legs. One time we got tangled up and both tumbled. It wasn't a foul, just a good, hard

struggle for space. A frown cast a shadow across Tony's face. The first-minute goal had been great, but running a marathon to find space without getting a touch of the ball obviously wasn't his idea of fun. Also he was under pressure from all the scouts watching. He hadn't had a kick in fifteen minutes.

Half an hour passed, Nosher had made five saves from long range shots. Sam hit a curler from outside the penalty area, Nosh just got one hand to it. The ball lobbed straight up in the air and landed on the roof of the net. The corner found Ranjeet's head but Nosher's safe hands made a clean catch.

Villa hadn't had a shot at goal but we were defending strongly. Shots over the top of the defence didn't seem to bother Nosher and some of the Cale Green forwards had started to argue with each other.

Meanwhile, at the other end, Pete ran and ran and ran but Sam gobbled up everything. Both sides were bogged down but, of course, Cale Green were winning.

At almost half-time, it was Tony's turn to

make a mistake. He went very deep into his own half to try to lose me. However, this took me closer to Cale Green's goal than I had been at any time in the match.

Sam started one of his attacking gallops but pushed the ball too far ahead. Oggy won a fifty-fifty ball with him and lashed the ball at Pete. I ran wide right. Now it was Tony's turn to chase. Sam was stranded. There was a gap down the middle and only Tony to fill it. Two against one. Pete or me? He had to choose!

He chose me. I pulled to the right. Tony started to move with me.

Wrong!

Pete kept on going and hammered the ball past the advancing keeper.

GOAL! One-one!

Cale Green looked at the bench as the whistle went. This wasn't how things were supposed to turn out at all. The Cale Green manager waved his arms and pointed, red-faced, angry. The team hung their heads. That is, all except Tony who stared across at me with hard eyes and a determined expression.

'Sorry about the first one!' said Oggy.

'I was the one who lost him,' I said.

'Well done, lads! You've got them going,' said Jock Lindsay.

Next thing, Nick Doogan popped up.

'Watch Sam,' said Doogan. 'Because you're covering Tony and Ranjeet so tightly, he's finding space for these direct runs. He could do to you what Peter did to them.'

Second half and down came the cold needles of hail. Fifteen minutes passed and the game was

114

getting very scrappy. It was becoming a stalemate in midfield with Cale Green pressing and Villa hanging on. The first half was like a hurricane. Now all that fire was gone and legs were getting heavy on the massive City pitch.

Then, as the ball swung out to the Cale Green right wing, I tripped and Tony was gone again. He was amazing. Nothing had gone right for him for over half an hour yet, given the slightest chance, he had ghosted away effortlessly. Oggy was after him and I ran towards my own goal as fast as I could. Tony flicked the ball out to Ranjeet. Ranjeet made a storming run down the wing to cut the ball back to Tony.

Oggy was sliding in, leg out, to block the shot. I was sprinting behind him and Nosher was peering at it all between the posts.

Tony did a beautiful pull-back and left us standing. WHAP! Oggy, me and Sunil were leaping across to block, then fell spectacularly in the mud.

CRUNCH!

OOO! There was a great shout from the crowd. Where was the ball?

It had come off Sunil's boot and my shoulder and flown away over Nosher's head to bounce *twice* on top of the bar before rolling over for a corner.

Phew! Still one-one.

On and on we ploughed, deeper and deeper into the midfield mud. It was hard to turn quickly but, even so, Tony was a wriggly eel. Then another mistake.

Sam made yet another brilliant run. Tony sprinted hard towards his own goal to lose me. But, when Sam played the ball square, it stuck short in the mud. Now Tony had to race me for the ball. I was faster but he had a start. Ten metres, five, and in we both slid. Crunch! Neither of us pulled out and neither

won it cleanly. We both crumpled to the floor twisting and turning in pain. Sam sportingly lashed the ball out of play and waved madly to the bench.

Electric shocks ran up and down my left leg and my foot felt numb. I was up first. Tony didn't look good at all. I dragged myself across to where he was sitting.

'Right ankle,' said Tony.

'He'll have to go off,' said one of their lads.

'No. No.' Tony got to his feet pulling a terrible face. 'I'll be all right. Give us the spray.'

I didn't say a thing about how terrible I felt.

'You sure, son?' The referee looked carefully at Tony.

'Yeah!'

Villa threw the ball back to Cale Green and the last fifteen minutes began.

Pete sprinted, Ranjeet stormed and Oggy ran and ran but Tony and I doddered like two old Grandads on an afternoon stroll by the bowling green. Each of us was watching the other, each of us wondering if the other was fooling. Maybe Tony would make a fantastic burst. Maybe, he would stop the trickery and do something brilliant. If he did, it would be all over for us.

Ten minutes to go and I found out the truth. Sunil made a fast break out of defence and played yet another brilliant ball to Pete, but Sam was coming up fast. Peter shielded the ball and looked for support.

I started to stomp upfield with a pain worse than a thousand toothaches up my left leg. Tony was nowhere! I was biting my lip with pain as I hobbled.

Sam took the ball off Pete and a terrible feeling of panic ran all over me. The ball was floating over my head for Tony! Sunil, too, was stranded upfield in support.

Now there was a huge gap in our defence. Ranjeet was prowling like a wolf on the edge of the box. One magic touch and we're in trouble I thought but, as I struggled back, the ball skidded past Tony and out.

'We're both two old crocks today!' Tony said with a painful smile. 'I think I might have broken my ankle!'

'I just can't feel my foot!' I winced. 'Some

dream final!'

In no time at all, I waved Oggy forward.

'Tony's had it. I'll stay back. I just can't run any more.'

Oggy went wide on the right.

With five minutes to go, Sam made *another*

stop in the heart of the Cale Green defence. I had backed off a little. Whap! The ball found Tony. He whirled left, no slip this time, and left me for dead. This was the end! Ranjeet raced ahead. But three strides on Tony crumpled to the ground in pain.

In two seconds, I had clipped the ball to Oggy on the right wing. In three, I was running, stomping, hopping on my dead left leg towards Cale Green's near post. Oggy slowed. Pete was calling from the far post. Sunil was coming through fast on the edge of the area.

I hammered on. AAAH! Every step was torture. Stop! Stop! Stop! My body was screaming, but my legs kept battling on as I ploughed towards the goal.

Think JOE! JOE! JOE!

Oggy raced right round the left flank of the tired defence, into the area, right to the line. Then he tripped as he hit the ball and it looped towards the near post.

I wasn't quite there. Pete was too far back and the keeper was stranded between the two of us. The rest of the defence was racing back to help.

I could see the ball coming, a shiny, slippery snowball, curling just out of reach. To the right, the yellow blur of the keeper was coming up fast.

Straight in like Joe!

I dived but didn't take off at all, my leg gave way as I hurled myself. The ball smashed me full in the mouth and nose, cannoned off the

keeper's chest and landed in the mud on the Cale Green line. Pete won the chase and he, the ball, the keeper, two defenders and Sunil all ended up sliding into the back of the net together. GOAL! Two-one!

'YEHHH!' Ten of Villa's team were shouting as I dug myself out. At once, hands were dragging me up, slapping me on the back.

'Great ball, Sean!'

'Nice one, Pete!' I said.

Tony shook his head in disbelief as he limped by with a pained expression on his face.

I tried to speak but my mouth wouldn't work.

'You all right?' asked the referee.

'It's okay, ref. I'll die later!' I replied.

The next five minutes were very tense. Cale Green hurled themselves at us. They just wouldn't accept defeat. But, without Tony's genius, it was all in vain and the final whistle brought the game to an end.

All Villa's team except me turned into raving maniacs. I was so far gone I couldn't have raved to save my life. Me and Tony were like two jellyfish for the final five minutes. We were exhausted.

We helped each other off. Salty blood had started to trickle down my nose and into my mouth. I spat it out but the gritty mud crunched in my teeth.

'Well played, Drac,' grinned Tony. 'How's your foot?'

'All I need now is a parrot! How's your ankle?'
I asked.

'Same. Can't hardly feel it.'

Suzie came racing over to hug me. 'Oh, Sean, your leg! That was fantastic but . . . !'

'Good job *I'm* not dancing in the show!' I laughed as Suzie gave me a kiss.

'Nothing for me, then?' complained Tony with a grin.

Suzie smiled. Then she turned to me. 'Did you see Mum? She says she's coming to my show as well. She wants to see us on our own!'

Then I saw Dad and Joe coming to congratulate us.

Joe looked down at Tony and me.

'Are you two hard nuts or what? If you're like this now what will you be like when you're twenty-one?'

'You were hammering away like that when you were five, Joe!' said Dad. 'I've still got the stud marks!'

'Still,' said Joe. 'When you two are both playing for United, you can stop killing each other!'

The United scouts had liked what they had seen of Tony and me and they had decided to give us both a trial, when our injuries had healed. We were checked out and neither of us had broken anything after all. Both of us received our medals and Sam Leeson won the 'Man of the Match' award.

Finally, Joe told us his news. 'What a week! Guess what, City have given me a free transfer and Rochdale want me. New start, eh?'

Joe was leaving! But as he said goodbye, he promised to come and see us. Then he took me aside. 'You're going to make it, son,' he said to me quietly, so nobody else could hear. 'Believe me, you'll be better than your dad ever was!'

I looked at him, puzzled. 'What do you mean?' I said.

He looked at me hard. 'I think you know what I mean,' he said simply. 'I haven't been much use all your life so far – but I want you to know that if you ever need me I'll be there.' He turned and walked away. Tall, with the dark, curly hair so like my own. I watched him leave and yes, I understood at last.

About the Author

Sport, especially football, has played a big part in my life. When I was a child it took me from terraced streets to big open parks and great stadiums like Wembley. Even as an adult, the roar of a football crowd bursting like thunder has always thrilled me.

It seems to me that even if things aren't working out well, a sports pitch can be your Field of Dreams, just as it was for Sean.